Hush!

Written by Liz Miles

Illustrated by Elif Balta Parks

Collins

3

Josh has a den.

A duck runs in!

Chicks run in.

A big thing thuds.

Josh runs.

Josh has a posh den.

Hush!

/ch/

/qu/

After reading

Letters and Sounds: Phase 3

Word count: 39

Focus phonemes: /j/ /qu/ /ch/ /sh/ /th/ /ng/

Common exception word: the

Curriculum links: Understanding the World: The World

Early learning goals: Reading: use phonic knowledge to decode regular words and read them aloud accurately; demonstrate understanding when talking with others about what they have read

Developing fluency

- Model saying the sound effects with expression. For example: **hush**, **bang**, **quack**, **peck**.
- Encourage your child to sound talk and then blend each of the words, e.g. qu/a/ck **quack**. It may help to point to each sound as your child reads.
- Then ask your child to reread the sentence with expression to support fluency and understanding.

Phonic practice

- Ask your child to tell you which words have a /sh/ sound in:
  - chops ship duck sink posh fish shock (*ship*, *posh*, *fish*, *shock*)
- Look at the "I spy sounds" pages (14–15) together. Discuss the picture with your child. Can they find items/ examples of words that use the /ch/ and /qu/ sounds? (e.g. *torch*, *chimpanzee*, *chest*, *chair*, *bench*, *quilt*, *quack*, *quiet*)

Extending vocabulary

- Ask your child:
  - What words could you use instead of **hush** when asking someone to be quiet? (e.g. *shush*, *be quiet*, *be silent*, *be soundless*, *be noiseless*)
  - Can you think of any words to describe a loud noise? (e.g. *bang*, *thud*, *thump*, *boom*, *crash*, *smash*, *roar*, *clatter*, *clang*)
  - Sort the following words into loud noises and quiet noises:

  bang clatter whisper murmur boom crash buzz hum (*loud – bang*, *clatter*, *boom*, *crash*; *quiet – whisper*, *murmur*, *buzz*, *hum*)